TRUE | **FALSE**

Can You HANDLE THE TRUTH?

by **Kecia A. Johnson**
art by Lindsey Bailey

Can You Hande the Truth? by Kecia A. Johnson
The Kiojah and Lee Book Series, Book 2

ISBN (softcover): 978-1-7360735-2-0
ISBN (ebook): 978-1-7360735-3-7
Library of Congress Control Number: 2020924929

Illustrations by Lindsey Bailey
Book design by Jill Ronsley, suneditwrite.com
Ebook by Sun Editing & Book Design

Published by Acacia's Ark LLC
keciajohnson.com

10 9 8 7 6 5 4 3 2 1

Printed and bound in the USA

To dear family and friends, who are my buttress,
to chosen and precious children,
and to my Lord and Savior Jesus Christ,
all my love and sincere appreciation

Twins Kiojah and Lee Hughes
live in a make-believe town in Florida.
They take turns telling this story in every chapter,
each from their own point of view.

In this way, they give the reader
a peek into their family life
and an all-access pass to the fifth grade
at River Forest Elementary School.

Contents

Good Teammates

"Aw, man! Jimmie, look what you did," Luke said, laughing.

Luke was soaked by the water that had burst out of the now empty bottle in his hands.

"I was just tryin' to help ya' out. Guess I squeezed this here thing too hard," Jimmie said, turning red while still holding the spray nozzle.

"I didn't ask for help, you big, strong, super—"

"Excuse me. What are you two doing out of your seats?" Ms. Ferguson asked, turning her focus to the sink at the back of the classroom. "What signal are you supposed to give me when you want to get a drink of water?"

Suddenly, loosened by the blast, the poster showing the hand signals for restroom, tissue, and water slipped off the wall. Everyone in the class laughed.

"Team! Team!" Ms. Ferguson said.

"Yes, yes," we all replied as we sat back down in our seats. Ms. Ferguson had our attention again.

"I'd like to introduce you to a new member of our team, Yanick Bailey," she said.

Yanick was wearing the latest pair of high-top sneakers that had been released in stores the previous week. He had on a matching T-shirt and baseball cap and would soon find out that he'd have to take off the cap in the classroom.

"Our new teammate comes from Reigns Elementary School," Ms. Ferguson continued.

Yanick stood proud with his head held high, like a king. Most of the boys and girls who went to Reigns were known for being either awesome at sports or tough and aggressive. There was a silent sense of wonder in the entire room as everyone looked around. Whispering broke the shock. Most of the girls whispered because he was cute.

"Mr. Bailey will be sitting next to Kiojah," Ms. Ferguson said.

There was an empty desk right next to me. I was quiet in class, but Ms. Ferguson knew that I was helpful to my teammates. I was also good at welcoming people who were new to our school—even grown-ups.

Before Yanick could take the first step towards his seat, Fallon yelled across the room, "I don't think it's fair."

Everyone, including Ms. Ferguson and Yanick, looked surprised. Ms. Ferguson did not like it when we shouted out in class.

"Excuse me, Fallon, but what should you do if you have something to say in class?"

"I should raise my hand." She raised her right hand.

Ms. Ferguson nodded, letting her know it was okay to speak.

"I don't think it's fair that you seat the new kids in Kiojah's row," she said, standing up. "Plus, Lee and the kids in her row just got in trouble for being rude when the substitute was here. I don't think that's a good example for Yanick."

"Don't try to shine on me," my twin brother, Lee, said. He was sitting in timeout next to the teacher's desk at the back of the classroom. "Ms. Ferguson knows what's up. I was sitting in that seat, but the sub was rude to me first. He kept calling me the wrong name."

"Fallon is always being shady," Jordan called out. "She's throwing shade, but she'd better be ready to throw some hands."

"Team! Team!" Ms. Ferguson said loudly, raising her hand.

"Yes, yes," we all said, raising our hands.

"Lee, I already had to call your mom on Monday. Keep this up, and I will be calling her again tonight.

And Jordan, making threats is unacceptable. Today you will have timeout during recess. Is that clear?"

"Yes, ma'am," Jordan said.

"Fallon," Ms. Ferguson continued. "I know about everything that happened with the substitute. I don't need you to remind me, nor do I need you to tell me where to seat new students."

Yanick shook his head and put his designer GymSport backpack on the desk. He sat down next to me and pulled out a pen and a notebook.

I looked at Yanick, smiled, and said, "Hey, welcome to River Forest."

I noticed that the designs in his haircut matched his shirt and his backpack. Now that was cool.

"*Tanks*," he said.

"I'm Kiojah." I turned and pointed behind me. "This is my friend, Areebah." I pointed to the other side of Yanick. "That's Jordan, one of my best friends."

Areebah asked, "Hey, may I help you set up your laptop? I can get a new one for you from the cart."

"Sure," he said.

Ms. Ferguson walked over to our group. "Kiojah, if you don't mind, I would like you to help Yanick get used to our school. After school, he will be a walker with you guys. Will you let him walk with you today so that he learns our routines for leaving campus?"

I knew she was actually telling me what to do, not asking.

Yanick looked at us and smiled. "We moved up yah fram down sout. We live in de apartments right acrass de street fram River Forest," he said.

We were shocked by his accent. He may have moved from another part of our state, but he was not from our state.

"*Yaaasss*, for this accent," Jordan said so loudly that the whole team became silent. "I'm sorry, where were you born?" he asked quietly, hunching his shoulders. We all knew he wasn't sorry for blurting anything out.

"Me family originally fram Jamrock. Me taak Patois an English."

"Jam-*what*?"

"Jamrock. Yuh know? Jamaica. Now me mudda is a student at de university yah. Kiojah, Weh yuh seh?"

"When we leave school, we cross the street in front of the apartments where you live," I explained to him. "If you want, we can walk home from school together."

"Sure," Yanick said.

Areebah came back and put the new laptop down in front of Yanick. He opened it, typed his username and password, and waited.

"This is how you access our team's website," Areebah said, turning her laptop to face him. "You see, Edulink is a portal that lets you use all the digital stuff that the school says is okay for kids to use. There are some lit games on here, too. Did you use this at your old school?"

Yanick shook his head. "Neva."

Areebah helped him organize his Oodle Drive— a file storage system for kids—which is what Ms. Ferguson wanted the team to use to keep track of the work we did in class. Areebah was good with technology. Ever since the first time Ms. Ferguson showed her how to use online tools to organize our work, she'd been training all the other kids to use them.

"Let's settle down, team," Ms. Ferguson said. "Today's date is December 8th, and our topic for language arts is 'What happens when a dream is deferred, or takes a long time to come true?' Our standard today requires us to compare and contrast two poems about dreams that were written by Langston Hughes, a leading thinker and writer during the Harlem Renaissance. Lee, will you read our essential questions?"

Lee cleared his throat, stood up at the timeout desk, and straightened his collar. He was so extra sometimes. I knew he was proud because our last name was Hughes.

Lee read the question like a college professor. "How does Langston Hughes use words or phrases in the poems to express emotions to the reader?"

"Please open up your first Oodle document, and we will begin there," Ms. Ferguson said.

I leaned over to help Yanick, because he was looking all over the class page for the link. With a few clicks, he was into the assignment. I knew we were going to be good teammates.

For the rest of the day Jordan, Areebah, and I helped Yanick get used to everything. We showed him all the people and places he would need to know on campus. At 3:00, he looked at me and said, "Ki, me wanna tank yuh for helpin' today. May me call yuh Ki?"

"Yes, and you're welcome," I said, smiling.

"Me feelin' dis school, yuh know," he said, smiling back at me.

Jordan said, "That's the bell. Let's go."

Instead of being in a nice line, our team was a messy huddle, waiting to give Ms. Ferguson a high five, a handshake, or a hug before leaving the classroom.

Outside, the warmth of the sun felt so good after sitting in the air-conditioned classroom most of the day. Yanick stopped, took off his hoodie, and put it in his backpack while we waited for him near the crossing guard. Ms. Nina greeted him with a big squeeze as she welcomed him to our neighborhood.

Ms. Nina lived in a red brick house up the street and had been the crossing guard for a long time.

Even my older cousins knew her. We only saw her briefly before and after school. She was like cotton candy—always giving just enough sweetness before she disappeared.

A group of us stood at the corner, saying, "Left, right, left—look over your shoulder!" which is what Ms. Nina made us say while we looked up and down the street to see if it was clear for crossing. Even though she would blow the whistle to stop the cars, Ms. Nina wanted to train us to watch for cars when we were away from school. After we had crossed, Yanick gave me a high five.

"Yanick, this is my twin brother, Lee," I said.

"Wah gwan, twin!" Yanick said as he gave Lee a fist bump.

We walked together for a little while before Yanick crossed the street and the big open field in front of the new apartment complex. A beautiful woman with the longest braids I'd ever seen kissed Yanick's cheek and rubbed his hair. I wondered if that was his mother.

Lee and I waited for Sofia.

"Hola, amigos. ¿Cómo están?" She greeted us in her usual quiet way. Sofia must have found out that she was supposed to walk home with us. She only walked on the days when her dad didn't have a class.

"We're cool," Lee said, and he started to tell Sofia about his day.

I wanted to talk to Sofia so I could practice Spanish. I could almost have a full conversation in Spanish about normal stuff, but not school stuff.

We were getting close to Ms. Meanie's house. We honestly didn't know the old lady's name, but we called her Ms. Meanie because she was so mean. She had a beautiful white and pink house. If Ms. Meanie's yard were someone's head, no hair would be out of place. It looked like she cut the grass with scissors and shaped the bushes with a cookie cutter.

On sunny days, the bright white spray paint covering her whole driveway and the sidewalk in front of her home, matching her bright white house, was blinding. All that white paint was broken up by pink shutters, a pink door, and pink trim around the roof. It looked like it should be on a TV show for kids.

We tiptoed while peering around to see if the coast was clear to walk on the sidewalk in front of Ms. Meanie's yard. I glanced at Lee. He gave a thumbs-up. I checked with Sofia, and she whispered, *"No veo a la viejita."*

We grabbed the straps of our backpacks and sprinted towards the spray-painted pavement.

2

The Best Gifts

We were destroyed! At that very moment, Ms. Meanie poked her head out from behind a bush. "Get off my sidewalk! Walk around! How many times do I have to tell you?" she screamed in a crackling voice.

Sofia continued to run towards our house at the end of the street.

"*Daaang!*" Jordan yelled. "I thought trolls lived under bridges, not in cute houses." He stomped the dirt from his shoes in the middle of the spotless driveway and ran to catch up with the rest of us.

Why? Why would Ms. Meanie paint the whole sidewalk and driveway white? I mean, didn't she know that the sidewalk was free for everybody to use? This was the kind of stuff grown-ups did that made me so angry. Honestly, I got in trouble a lot because grown-ups just didn't understand kids. This incident reminded me of what had happened yester-day in class.

When I was just sitting in my seat, I blurted out, "What? That wasn't even me." I looked at Kiojah. She knew I was wondering why Ms. Ferguson always blamed me for everything. All I'd done was laugh out loud.

We were in science, studying how the interactions between wind, water, and land create weather conditions and patterns. We were mostly talking about precipitation and the water cycle. Luke and Jimmie ended up arguing about whether or not climate change was causing more precipitation on Earth.

Luke said, "Well, I must be a meteorologist, because I predict a ninety-five percent chance of showers every time Jimmie opens his mouth."

I laughed out loud.

Jimmie's embarrassment morphed into upset. According to Ms. Ferguson, it was my fault that Luke and Jimmie were arguing—but I was just laughing because it tickled me. Everybody knows Jimmie "sprinkles" when he talks with those braces on his teeth. I got sent to timeout.

The previous day while I was working with Jimmie, suddenly, light "raindrops" fell on our worksheet. I was like, "Come on, man." Ms. Ferguson moved *me*.

Mama always said I needed to control my behavior and be respectful, no matter how other people behaved. That was why I decided not to even tell

Mama about the Ms. Meanie situation. In conflicts between an adult and me, Mama sided with the adult ninety-nine percent of the time. The situation with Meanie would only get me into more trouble.

The next day in school I was free from timeout and back in my normal seat. I planned to try hard to show self-control and pulled out my notebook to get ready for class.

Ms. Ferguson said, "Okay, team, yesterday we had some unsportsmanlike conduct. Remember, one rule of the game around here is that we respect our teammates at all times."

She pointed to a poster of a referee blowing a whistle. The words of our classroom contract were printed in a bubble next to the whistle. Ms. Ferguson said, "Do you think we can play by the rules today? From now on, whenever we have a team huddle or discussion, I will post some sentences on the board. For example, when you do not agree with someone, you can say 'I disagree with Areebah because ...' This is better than saying 'That's a lie.'"

The whole team laughed, and I chuckled to myself while Ms. Ferguson gave more examples.

My mind wandered and I looked around the classroom. I noticed Yanick. I could tell he was into fashion, so we might end up talking about what's in style.

Last night I was surfing online when I found an article about the environment and precipitation. I read it and even took a little quiz. Then I felt ready for a debate.

Luke came over to my desk and pointed towards Kiojah and Yanick. I looked and shrugged my shoulders. "So what?"

"Look."

I looked again.

"Man, Yanick is spending a lot of time with your sister."

I was annoyed.

"Whatever Kiojah has going on, that's the last thing I'm worried about."

Sometimes people wanted me to care about everything Kiojah did because she was my twin, but we were still two different people.

Mama always told us, "Remember, you're your twin's keeper. When you were born with a twin, God gave you one of the best gifts."

At the beginning of the school year, I got sick with juvenile arthritis. My joints ached so much, but Kiojah was right there. She always asked me if I needed anything. When I could barely walk, she made sure nobody bumped into me at school. On my bad days, she carried my backpack. Kiojah was a quiet person who did not stand up for herself, but I knew she was down for me.

The morning went by fast, and our team got ready to go to lunch. Everyone was excited, because today we had recess right after lunch. We could sit wherever we wanted at our table, so I sat by Jimmie and Sofia. Luke and Fallon sat down across from us.

Fallon was cool and smart, but she was all about herself. Some kids didn't like that about her. I would sometimes have to put Fallon in her place, but I didn't have a problem with her. That day she went on and on about all the cool stuff she was buying her mom for Christmas.

"Most importantly, my mom bought me a pre-Christmas gift," she said, holding up her arm to show off a silver Xaria charm bracelet.

That made me wonder what Kiojah and I could give our parents for Christmas.

After a conversation about the best Christmas gifts, I stood up to throw away my trash. Our team had already started lining up. I was always one of the last people to finish eating because I had to wait for the kitchen staff to microwave Mama's home-cooked food.

As soon as I stepped out of the cafeteria, Luke came running up to me, laughing. "Man, look!" he said.

Yanick was with Kiojah under the big tree in the playground. I saw him give her a little box and said, "I wonder what's in that—"

"A set of earbuds," Luke blurted out before I could finish my sentence. "Look at how the box is shaped. No, it's one of them little robots. Man, it's a candy ring. They're getting married, Lee."

I cracked up. "You are out of control."

I thought about it for a few seconds. Most days I didn't care what Kiojah did with her little friends, but this box had me curious. I looked at Luke. "You have a point. Let's wait until Yanick is not around to ask Kiojah what's up."

We heard Ms. Ferguson's whistle and ran to her.

"It's time for your favorite part of the day—math," she announced.

Half of the team said, "Yes!" but the other half were sad because math wasn't their thing.

I hoped we would have a fun lab—like the time we learned about fractions and percent and used little colored chocolates to build charts; after we'd looked for patterns in each of the colors, we got to eat them.

At the end, we either skipped, walked fast, hopped, or even danced back into the classroom since it was against the rules for us to run at school. When we stepped into the classroom, a bad smell busted me right in the nose. Some of our teammates just didn't know how to use deodorant or take a shower.

Today I was excited about math because I was in Kiojah's group, and I would be able to find out what was up with that gift. I saw her quietly slip the little box into her backpack. Ha! She thought she was slick.

The room was filled with a loud screeching of tables and chairs being moved and the sound of backpacks being opened and closed. Finally, we were in our math groups.

I got right to the point. "Kiojah, I know you gonna show me what's in that box."

"Lee, what are you talking about?"

"Oh, you know what's going on." I laughed.

Areebah smiled and giggled. "What box?" she asked. "Kiojah girl, you got secrets? I wanna know too."

We both stared at Kiojah. She smiled.

"All right, all right. Yanick gave me a box, and it has a gift in it," she said. She looked around to see if anyone could hear us.

"You got a boyfriend," Areebah said. "You didn't tell us!"

I didn't want to hear all the details. I just wanted to know what was in the box. "What's in the box, Kiojah? Let me see."

"I'll let you see, but on our way home. I don't want to take it out now. It's a bracelet."

"A bracelet! What kind of bracelet?" I blurted out. I looked around to see if anyone had heard me and decided to whisper. "It must be one of those bracelets you make with all those colorful little rubber bands."

"No, Lee, it's a *rose gold* bracelet. It's a real bracelet."

"Well, you know Justice Hughes is not gonna let you keep that." Justice is our mom's name.

"We'll see."

Areebah giggled again.

Ms. Ferguson said, "Okay, team, for today's mental workout we will see what happens when we divide when using fractions. In your teams you will come up with two stories or word problems that involve dividing fractions."

Areebah looked at Kiojah. "Well, if your mom won't let you keep the bracelet, how about you just keep it in your backpack and put it on when you come to school? If somebody bought me a nice bracelet, I would find a way to keep it and wear it."

I was done with the bracelet talk. I already had good ideas for our math problem.

"A school club needs T-shirts," I said. "One T-shirt takes seven-tenths of a meter of fabric. How many T-shirts can be made from forty meters of fabric?"

I liked to work fast in group work. It gave us more time to talk when we finished. That day, making up our own word problems took longer than I expected, and we finished just in time for the end of school. The bell rang. The class was loud again. Everyone pushed chairs, slammed books and notebooks onto desks, and zipped up backpacks and jackets. After all that, we waited silently in a messy line in front of

Ms. Ferguson, who stood at the door. Every day we entered and exited the classroom in the same way.

"Okay, time for a handshake, a high five, or a hug," Ms. Ferguson said as we left.

We walked towards Ms. Nina at the crosswalk, crossed the street, and kept going to the apartments. Yanick waved goodbye to Kiojah and she waved back.

Right away I said, "Let me see it."

Jordan and I waited while she opened the box. She laughed and pulled out the gift.

"Girl, he gave you that? I wouldn't have given you nothin' that fancy," Jordan said with a smirk before Kiojah could say a word.

She gave him an evil stare.

"Wow, Kiojah, that's a nice Xaria bracelet. It's almost the same as Fallon's new bracelet," I said.

We kept walking until we reached the snow-white sidewalk in front of Ms. Meanie's house. In the afternoon sun we needed to wear shades just to look at it. It was beyond bright. I was sure Ms. Meanie wasn't around until I spotted her hat poking out near one of the tall bushes at the corner of the house. She was standing on a stool with a string of Christmas lights in her hands.

Before we could warn each other, she growled, "How about you go around? You know the drill."

I started to say something, but Kiojah stopped me. "Lee, it's not worth it."

Meanie stepped off the stool and glared at us.

Jordan said, "Okay. I got her. I got her."

"Come on Jordan, let's go around," I said.

We walked around Ms. Meanie's sidewalk and watched her from the other side of the street. She'd hung white Christmas lights, making her house look like some kind of winter palace. She knew it was fire, and she didn't want kids like us to mess it up.

Jordan said, "If she yells at us again, I bet I can make sure she shuts her mouth every time she sees kids on her sidewalk."

Kiojah and I looked at each other in silence and just kept walking until he turned to go to his house.

The smell of salmon patties massaged my nostrils when I entered our house. Mama had made it home, and she was in the kitchen banging the pots and pans with Nana. I was glad Nana had come to live with us. Most nights my daddy wasn't home for dinner. He would eat alone after coaching his team at their basketball practice. Sometimes I would shower and help because I loved to cook.

That night Mama and Nana had prepared rice and okra for dinner. We sat around the table and bowed our heads.

"God is great. God is good. Let us thank Him for our food," I said. Short and to the point.

"Amen," everyone said.

Mama asked, "How was your day?" just as she always did. I told her how my ideas for word problems during math were the best.

"Lee, remember what I told you about that?" Mama asked. "Your work just needs to be *your* best."

Then Mama went there ...

"You haven't been back in timeout, have you?" she asked, putting her fork down.

"No ma'am," I said, using my fork to stir my rice and okra.

"Good. I send you to school to learn and have fun—not to be a clown. If someone else is cutting up, you still need to behave. And if someone—even an adult-—is giving you a hard time, you need to tell me. Understood?"

I nodded my head in agreement because my mouth was stuffed with rice and okra.

Kiojah couldn't keep a secret and pulled the bracelet out of the box.

"Mama, a boy gave me this today," she said.

"What?" Ma asked. Ma was always so dramatic. She would hear what we said and still ask us to repeat it.

Nana was silent.

Kiojah passed it to Ma.

Ma showed it to Nana.

"Kiojah, why did the boy want to give you this?" Mama asked.

Silence.

"Do his parents know he gave this to you?"

Silence.

If Kiojah didn't say something, Ma would ask a million questions.

"I don't know, Ma," Kiojah said.

I knew that Kiojah would have to come up with something better. Ma was going to grill her.

"You don't know?"

"Maybe because he's new to the school. Ms. Ferguson sat him by me because she knows I'm helpful. I'm showing him the school and introducing him to everybody there."

I shook my head.

"Agh! Get over it, Kiojah," I blurted out. "Nobody gives you that kind of stuff unless they like you."

Ma gave me a sharp look. Turning to Kiojah, she said, "You know that you are not allowed to have a boyfriend or accept this kind of gift. Do you think his mom knows that he gave you this expensive bracelet?"

I shook my head but didn't say anything this time. I wasn't crazy.

"I think he said his mom bought it for him to give to me because she said that he could have a girlfriend."

"What I'm telling you is that *you* cannot have a boyfriend. Kiojah, you need to take this bracelet back to that boy and let him know."

I know my sister, so I looked at her and said, "So what are you going to do?"

"Well, I'll thank him and give it back to him tomorrow at school," she said as she slowly moved the box down to her lap.

We finished dinner and I just wanted to crash. As soon as I lay down to go to sleep, I heard knocking on my door.

"Rise and shine. Give God the glory," Ma sang.

I put my head back down on the pillow and turned away from the light.

"Lee, get up. It's time for you to go to school. You slept for nine hours," Ma said.

It had been nine hours, but I felt like I'd only had a nap. I was quiet on the way to school because I was still waking up. We pulled into the front car circle and Ma dropped us off.

"I love you," she said.

"Love you too," I mumbled, and we were on our way.

We went straight to the cafeteria, where everyone waited for their teachers to come to pick them up. I sat across from Kiojah at the table, and guess who came to sit next to her?

3

Soft Lies Versus
Hard Truths

"Wah gwan, Ki?" Yanick said.

"Hey," I said, my smile matching Yanick's.

Just as I remembered the bracelet, Yanick dropped the big question.

"How yuh likin' de bracelet?"

I looked at Lee.

"I ... I love it. It's beautiful. Thank you so much," I said like a robot.

I reached into the front pouch of my backpack, opened the small box, and put the bracelet on my wrist. I gave Lee a look like, *If you say something, I will grow another arm, a long arm, and hit you on the back of your head.*

Lee looked the other way. He left with Luke, who walked by.

I knew this was wrong, but I didn't want to hurt

Yanick's feelings. He might have thought my giving back the bracelet was mean.

Whew! I was glad that was over. And I was glad Lee hadn't said anything.

Tuesday was my favorite day of the week because we had PE. I was one of the first kids to be ready when Ms. Ferguson told us to line up.

On our way to the court, Fallon came over to me. "Hey Kiojah, how about you work with Ellie and me?"

I didn't have a group yet. Honestly, I just wanted to work with Areebah and Lee, but I didn't want to hurt Fallon's feelings.

"Sounds good," I said before I could give myself a chance to tell her the truth.

Fallon was bougie. Her nose was a flag she kept up in the air as a sign that she was better than other people. I knew working out with her would annoy Areebah, who always said Fallon was not my friend. That was true. I just knew if I wasn't nice to Fallon, our class would be in a civil war, with Fallon and her friends against me and my friends. That would be stupid.

As we reached the outside court, Coach Powers broke us up into warm-up groups. When I walked up with Fallon, my friends stared at me. I started our warm-up drills. Coach Powers cranked up the music. This was the best part of the week for me, so I tried to ignore my crew being upset with me.

I understood Areebah being upset because she was my real friend. We used to walk home together all the time before her family moved from our neighborhood. Mrs. Ibrahim, Areebah's mom, had invited me to stay for dinner several times. We ate shawarma, falafel, and koshari. At first, the smell of the food and spices were too different from what I ate at home. I didn't like it at all, but I got used to the taste of most of the Egyptian food. And Areebah knew I loved her.

Fallon needed my kindness, though. She was a beautiful girl with shiny, curly red hair. Her eyes were sometimes bright green and sometimes brown. She had freckles that looked like cinnamon sprin-kled over her cheeks and lips that always looked like she was wearing pink lip-gloss. Her nails were manicured every week when she went to the salon with her mom, and she had cute clothes. Some girls wished they were Fallon. Some followed her the way the twelve men in the Bible followed Jesus, and some girls hated her guts. Other people, like my friends, didn't like or hate her—they just stayed away.

While we were jumping rope and having a good time with Coach Powers, Fallon began to tell me what she and her older siblings were buying for their mother for Christmas. Their family had a lot of money, and Fallon usually went on and on about the cool stuff they did with it. I needed to talk to Lee about what we could do for our parents for Christmas. We didn't have as much money, but we could still make Christmas special for them. Some of the gift ideas Fallon had for her mother were amazing.

All of a sudden, Jordan blurted out, "Aw, don't nobody care 'bout that. Did anybody ask you to go on and on and brag about what you gonna get your mom?"

We stopped jumping rope. I stared at Jordan.

"Fallon, don't look at me like that," Jordan said and turned to me. "Kiojah, you don't have to hang out with her if you don't want to." He tossed his curls and left. I didn't even know he had been close enough to hear what Fallon was saying.

Fallon looked at me. "Wow, Kiojah, you have a bracelet just like mine. Mine was a pre-Christmas gift from my mom."

"That's cool."

"I mean, yours is a little different than mine. Don't worry, whenever you get some more charms yours will look better."

I didn't know what to say. Suddenly a few raindrops came out of nowhere, and a big cloud followed. Coach Powers blew the whistle, and we all ran for shelter under the covered part of the court.

The day passed, and soon it was almost time for us to go home. Ms. Ferguson was going over the homework assignment.

"Okay, you need to read the article about new laws that might help kids stop drinking soda and other sugary drinks. Think about what you read, answer the questions, and post to your group's discussion board."

The class screamed as we scraped desks across the floor, flipped chairs, and slammed them on top of the desks. When we were finally silent, Ms. Ferguson held the door open for a handshake, high five, or hug as we left the classroom.

Yes. We were finally free and in the sun. It was still nice and warm, even though the temperature was dropping. We walked to Ms. Nina's corner. We tried to cross the street, and she blew three quick whistles at all the cars that didn't stop. When they finally did, we went across.

I waved goodbye to Yanick.

"Tek care, Ki," he said, smiling. He was so nice.

Lee asked, "Did you tell him that you're not going to be wearing his 'boo bracelet'?"

"It is not a girlfriend bracelet. And no, I didn't get a chance to tell him."

"You didn't have a chance to tell Yanick? Or you did not *want* to tell him because you thought you would hurt his feelings? The longer you wear that bracelet, the weirder it will be if you have to give it back one day. Don't say I didn't tell you."

I hated when Lee was right, so I just became quiet. I decided that I would definitely tell Yanick the next day.

"I don't know why you talk to Fallon," Jordan broke in, his words flying out of his mouth like potato chips flying out of a bag when you struggle with it and it suddenly pops open.

There we go. His words were crunchy, hard, and wild.

"Jordan, we were just talking about what we would buy our parents for Christmas!" I said.

"No, she was braggin'. She didn't even let you talk, did she? No. You don't need to be friends with someone who don't even let you say a word."

I squinted and stared at him.

"Anyway, tomorrow I'm going with my brother, Caleb, to look around the mall," Jordan said. "See if your parents will let you come. He's a good driver."

"Okay, we will ask our parents," I said.

By that time, we were near the winter palace. The little woman was nowhere in sight. We looked at each other and took the first step. Holding our breath, we took the second step, tiptoed lightly across the bright white sidewalk as if we were walk-ing on a cloud, and giggled once we'd reached the other side.

"I'm so tired of having to sneak across this dumb sidewalk or having to walk all the way into the road," Jordan said. "Meet me outside your house ten min-utes before we go shopping tomorrow, and I'll let you know the plan. Okay?"

Before we could ask Jordan any questions, the pink and white house just coughed her up.

"How many times do I have to tell you to stay away from here?" the old lady fussed from the top of a ladder hidden by a tall bush growing up the side of her little castle. "I'm going to walk down to your mother's house and tell her you are messing up my property with your dirty little feet."

Lee was heated. "She is so disrespectful," he said.

"Lee, it's not worth it," I said.

Jordan was a different story. He couldn't con-trol himself. Whatever was in Jordan's mind always made it to his mouth. Whatever Jordan believed in his heart always made it to his fists. I guess this could mean Jordan was honest and brave. But I'm not sure if it's honest or brave for an eleven-year-old to yell back at an adult.

"Let's go, Jordan," I said, trying to stop him from disrespecting Ms. Meanie. "Remember, you have a plan."

Lee

4

Bad Neighbors

This morning, I was looking forward to school, because we were going to start a research project. Ms. Ferguson had us pull out our laptops to get on Oodle. Yesterday, I read about some experiments in which more than a thousand people were able to tell how a stranger was feeling just by listening to them talk. Apparently, when someone was talking, you could better understand what was up with them by listening to them than by watching their face. I wanted to do some digging on this to find more evidence.

I had just pulled up a good website when I heard Yanick ask Kiojah why she never wore the bracelet. She blanked out for a while and was saved when Ms. Ferguson started to talk.

"Okay, team, click the left-hand menu on your browser and open a new window so that we can go to Discovery Hub."

I saw Fallon coming towards me. "What are you researching?" she asked.

"I found this article about communication. It suggests that it might be easier to understand how another person thinks or feels if you close your eyes and just listen."

She changed the subject. "Kiojah told me that you haven't decided on a Christmas gift for your parents."

"I talked to Kiojah last night, and we have some nice gifts in mind. We just haven't shared them with you."

I could tell she wanted me to ask about what she planned to do for her parents. I acted like I was too busy with work to care. I did not want to have more words with Fallon than I had to.

Jordan interrupted. "Kiojah and Lee are going shopping with me and my brother, Caleb, today after school."

Sometimes Jordan could go overboard, but this time his sassy attitude saved me from having to talk to Fallon. She just looked at both of us, blinked her green eyes, and walked away.

Soon the best part of the week came—going to the media center. This month Ms. Patel, our media specialist, was teaching us about multicultural holidays that take place during wintertime. My family celebrated Christmas, but I enjoyed learning about Three Kings Day, Hannukah, Kwanzaa, and various

New Year's traditions. First, we watched a video about respecting winter holiday traditions from other cultures. Then we had a chance to break up into groups to work on short presentations we would make before the holiday break. Each group would teach the class about one winter holiday. Finally, we checked books out of the library. I didn't need to look for a new book. I renewed my loan and sat on a bright yellow foam cushion to read.

Before I knew it, it was time to go home. At the end of the day Ms. Ferguson had to yell because the team was out of control. Jordan stood up and twirled like a ribbon. Areebah had her phone out and was showing Kiojah a video of her brother singing at a holiday concert. Luke was running around, chased by another kid—that is, until he tripped. On his way down, he hit Fallon's pencil box, sending the pencils flying into the air. I just sat there shaking my head and laughing.

"Team! Team!" Ms. Ferguson yelled. I could tell she hated to raise her voice. She put her hand up and waited for us to be silent and put our hands up.

"Yes, yes," we replied.

"Do *not* run. Everyone, get your backpacks. Get your homework folder. Pack up and sit down. I do not want to hear one sound."

Finally, the bell rang, and we all looked at Ms. Ferguson. No one said a word.

When we'd made it outside, Jordan immediately talked about how Kiojah and I needed to put Fallon in her place. Kiojah and I discussed what we wanted for dinner and how we were looking forward to going to the mall with him and Caleb.

While we were on the "normal sidewalk," we saw Ms. Meanie stop working and stand up. Holding one of the big candy cane yard decorations in her hand, she glared at us. We moved off the sidewalk and walked on the street.

Jordan was smiling. It was weird. He said, "I got something for her. Some people have to learn their lessons the hard way. At least that's what my momma said."

"Jordan, what are you planning?" Kiojah asked.

"Meet me here at 5:45. It's going down," he said, staring back at Ms. Meanie.

"All right man, we'll see you in a few hours," I said, wondering what he was up to.

Kiojah said goodbye, and we walked home. The smell of food high-fived my nostrils when I walked in the door. I loved when Nana cooked something we could actually eat before we had real dinner. Today Nana had prepared greens and baked chicken wings. She'd also made corn bread from scratch in her cast-iron skillet. She must have been in a good mood because usually we got a peanut butter and jelly sandwich on wheat bread or a baked sweet potato. Today was a feast.

We ate, did our homework, and talked to Nana about the school day. Then we went outside to play a little basketball with some of the kids from around the block. A lot of kids liked coming to our house in the afternoons since our driveway had so much space to play. We argued about checking the ball, whether or not Kiojah had traveled on her layup (she had!), and if the shot I'd blocked was a foul (it was clean!). During the last argument, Kiojah looked at me with a look that said, "I'm tired." Since we could not have even teams without her, the rest of the crew decided to go home. We went back into the house, showered, and changed our clothes. It was almost time to meet Jordan.

The sun was setting, there was a cool breeze, and the neighborhood was quiet. We met Jordan at the corner of Ms. Meanie's yard. Most of the time her house was peaceful because she lived alone. The white lights neatly trimmed the house and made it look like a gingerbread castle.

Kiojah gasped, "Wow."

We only saw the house during the daytime because our momma didn't let us walk around the neighborhood after dark. Today she let us stay outside later since we were going to meet Jordan.

"This is so beautiful," Kiojah said.

Jordan said, "I am about to teach Ms. Meanie a lesson. We're good kids, but she thinks we're bad. I'll show her bad."

I twisted my face, about to say, "What are you talking about?" but before I could ask the question, he grabbed a handful of lights on the bush nearest to us and ripped them down. My mouth fell off my twisted face. This boy was crazy. Kiojah put both hands to her mouth. Her eyes were wide with amazement.

"That is for calling us dirty last week," Jordan announced, and as he pulled down a second string of lights, he exclaimed, "And this is for the time she put a sign out and blocked the sidewalk when she was spray-painting it."

What Jordan was doing was wrong, but at the same time it was kind of right. Maybe Meanie would leave us alone. I shook my head as he yanked a large candy cane out of the ground and broke it in half on his thigh. Suddenly I got angry thinking about all the times this mean old lady had disrespected us.

Kiojah and I went along with the thrill of revenge and charged the yard. From the side of the house we pulled down white lights that fell quietly from the roof like icing melting from a gingerbread castle. I knocked down her little candy canes and Kiojah followed suit. Jordan pushed over the inflated Santa and jabbed a hole in it with a sharp pencil.

I wondered where he'd got the pencil.

Meanie's fantastic Christmas display was ruined. To make things worse, Kiojah tracked dirt from her shoes onto the white driveway.

Suddenly, I said, "Man, let's go. It's time to go, or we're gonna get caught."

Not a moment later, we heard police sirens coming from the opposite end of the neighborhood.

Wrong + Wrong ≠ Right

Jordan grabbed one more handful of lights and threw them on the grass. We sprinted as fast as we could to the corner, where we bent over, trying to catch our breath.

"Man, my heart is thumping as if the FAMU drumline was inside my chest," Lee said.

I threw my hands above my head. "Oh my goodness! We know better than this," I said, breathing heavily.

Destroying Ms. Meanie's yard went against the "treat others the same way you want them to treat you" and the "do good to those who mistreat you" lessons we'd learned in church about how to be kind to a hater. It especially went against everything we had learned about how to respect adults.

Lee grabbed Jordan's shoulder. "Jordan! Man, are you crazy? Yeah, we know better than this, but we can't go back and fix it now."

I tried to make sense of what we had just done. "I know she's mean and sometimes she's even evil. It still ain't right for us to do that, Jordan," I whispered with a growing sense of fear.

This was a terrible thing that would be hard for me to get out of my mind.

Lee knew this. "Kiojah, just calm down. Everything will work out."

From a distance we saw Ms. Meanie running out of her house with tears in her eyes, pointing to the mess in her yard. While she talked to the police officers who had arrived on the scene, we rounded the corner near Jordan's house, jumped into Caleb's car, and waited for him to pull out.

The ride to the mall was quiet. Although Meanie had earned her nickname, we had become the mean ones. And I didn't like it.

A remixed Christmas rap song blasted. Even with Caleb's holiday playlist thumping through the speakers, I felt like everyone in the car could hear the bass sound of my heart beating inside my chest. I put my hand on my chest and felt the cross necklace Aunt Emily had given me for my birthday. It was as if Jesus was calling out to me, "Kiojah, I'm so sad about what you did."

Oh Lord, I'm so, so sorry, I prayed to myself.

"Get it together!" Lee said, staring at me.

I was so panicked I hadn't realized I was praying out loud.

"I know, I know ... I'm tryin'." I moved my hand away from the cross and covered my mouth. Ms. Meanie was a witch to us, but it still wasn't right for us to destroy her hard work.

Caleb heard us and said, looking in the rearview mirror, "Hey, what's going on back there? You guys okay?"

Jordan turned around and rolled his eyes at me.

Before we could answer, Caleb cranked up the music. We started turnin' up and enjoying ourselves. For a little while, I almost forgot about messing up Meanie's yard. This was supposed to be a fun time. I was on my way to hang out at the mall with Jordan and Lee on a school night.

"Lee, do you still have the money for our gifts?" I asked.

He leaned to the side and reached into his back pocket. His eyes looked surprised. It wasn't there.

"Oh, no! What if ..." I said.

"Calm yourself," he said, patting the left pocket on the front of his jean jacket.

"Whew! What if that wallet had fallen out of your pocket when we were going off in Meanie's yard?" I said fearfully.

"Chill! The first gift I want to look for is a nice watch for Daddy."

"No, let's get Mama's favorite perfume, because I saw that the Uncommon Scents store has new gift sets. Mama doesn't like many perfumes, so we should get her favorite one."

Lee agreed.

Caleb pulled up to the mall and drove around to find a parking space. He was in his second year of high school and was already captain of the football team. Last year, he was voted most popular freshman. He was in student government, and he even led the youth group at church.

Jordan could be a leader, too—just a different kind of leader. I think other kids didn't always understand him. Even though he was good at sports, most of the boys at school didn't choose him to be on their teams in PE, so he usually hung out with us girls. We didn't mind because he was so funny. The other day he took the sparkly clip out of Areebah's hair and pinned it in the curls that he had grown out like bangs. He wore that clip the whole day.

Caleb parked the car near the main entrance of the mall and we went to the Uncommon Scents store. Caleb told us to meet him at the front counter in twenty minutes, which would be at 6:30, and we agreed. Lee and I quickly opened the shopping lists on our phones.

Lee was a master shopper. He had a taste for the finer things that cost more money. This made him the best gift giver. However, I wanted to have enough money to buy gifts for all the people on our list. We found a gift set for Mama that came with a free travel bag. As we headed towards the cash register, we saw Caleb waiting and a police officer walk up behind him.

The lady behind the counter was yelling at Caleb, but I knew he would *never* do anything to get in trouble. I couldn't imagine why this lady was being so nasty to him.

"Officer Neel, please do not listen to anything this boy has to say," she screamed. "He was going to walk right out of the store without paying for his items. He's the one who has been stealing. He was here last week."

Jordan's brother looked at the police officer, and as he opened his mouth to speak, the lady cut him off.

"Look. You can tell he's up to no good," she said angrily. "Anybody who wears their hair that way—I know his kind. They come in here all the time without their parents. I catch them all the time."

The officer looked at the woman. He looked at Caleb.

"Now, son, wait a minute. Are you Brandon and Chelsea's boy?" Officer Neel asked.

Caleb nodded his head. "Yes, sir."

"I know this young man as a leader of youth services at our church, where I play basketball in a league with his dad," Officer Neel said to the woman behind the counter.

"So, were you near the front of the store when the alarm went off?" he asked Caleb.

Caleb looked up. "Yes, sir, I *was* over there looking at a gift set on display. But I did *not* take it out of the store. You have to believe me."

The woman came out from behind the counter. "You were here the other day. I know it was you. I know that hair when I see it. You were even wearing the same jeans," she yelled.

"Well, son, are your parents here? We will be looking at the video. If you were over there when the sensor went off—"

At that moment, his radio beeped, and a voice addressed him. "Breaker 1-9. Officer Neel, what's your 20?"

"The Uncommon Scents store," Officer Neel said.

"10-4," the voice said.

From the right, another officer was approaching, holding a struggling boy by his shirt collar and shoulder. They were accompanied by the mall security guard. The boy was about the same size as Caleb and wore a similar pair of jeans, except that Caleb's jeans were more torn. Both boys had on high-top sneakers, but their sweatshirts were not the same color. The other boy's hair was the same apart from the blonde-colored highlights on its ends.

"Officer Neel, this young man was caught running out of the Gym Shoes store," the officer said, huffing and puffing. "We found items with tags from this store in his pockets and in a shopping bag we confiscated. Glad you were already on the scene."

Officer Neel shook his head sadly. "Thank you," he said. He looked directly at the lady from Uncommon Scents and moved his eyes to Caleb.

"Hey, son, I'm sorry about all of this," he said. "I believed you."

The mall security guard added, "Yeah, we have been watching this young man on camera since the middle of last week. Alarms had gone off and items were missing from several stores. We wanted to see if the same guy was behind all the crimes. We sent out messages with his description to every store."

The saleswoman looked at Caleb. "I am *so* embarrassed. I am *so* sorry. I could have sworn it was you I saw. You boys look so much alike."

Not really, I thought. Caleb and Jordan's dad was Black, but their mom was White. Caleb had way lighter skin and eyes than the boy who had been arrested. The thief only wore the same style of clothing.

I looked at Lee. I could see he was upset. Jordan was silent, and this surprised me. Jordan was *never* silent.

Lee said, "Man," as if he was about to say something, but I shook my head.

The woman put her hand on Caleb's shoulder and said, "I'm the manager. When people steal, it makes my job harder and I get so angry. I was wrong for yelling at you. Will you forgive me?"

Caleb looked at her. "Ma'am, I accept your apology. No hard feelings. You were just doing your job. I'm glad you found out who had taken the things from the store."

"Hey, son, I'm going to give your dad a call tonight to let him know what happened," Officer Neel said. "Be safe and enjoy the rest of your night."

Caleb shook the officer's hand. We paid for our gifts as if nothing had happened and walked out of the store.

We were all in a state of shock. Jordan finally opened his mouth and ten thousand words spilled out at the same time.

"I can't believe you were just like, 'Ma'am, don't worry about it.' What? After she called you a thief? She talked about 'your kind,' and you know what she meant. She said you looked just like that boy. You don't have a bubble-shaped head like his. How could you let that racist woman get away with that?"

Lee cut him off. "Jordan, why didn't you say all this in the store? You froze—and you're never quiet."

"*I* was quiet? Lee, why didn't you say anything?"

"Because I had my cell phone out recording it all," Lee screamed. "You know I was not going to let somebody take Caleb down like that. I was being quiet so I could catch everything on video just in case we had to get a lawyer." He pointed his cell phone at Jordan.

Jordan and Lee were silent as we rode home in the car. I could tell they were thinking.

After a while, Lee said, "Man, I got this whole video on my phone. We can go right now to the police station. We can go right now to Channel 7 News. Let's upload it to FaceSpace and Snapblab."

Jordan cut in. "I saw at least three people from other high schools standing around there. Do you know what they will say? 'Look at Caleb over there stealing.' We can get this White lady in trouble for the way she treated you. White people always think Black kids are out to do something bad."

"Our mother is White. What are you talking about?" Caleb said.

"Mama doesn't count," Jordan snapped.

Why did Jordan say his mom didn't count as a White person? Did Ms. Ferguson count? She was definitely White. Even though their mom was White, Jordan and Caleb pretty much acted like all us Black kids.

"Hey, Jordan, just chill. You don't know everything," Caleb said. "Yes, the lady was mean. Yes, I was embarrassed. Yes, she was wrong for judging me based on how I look and for saying she saw me take the perfume. Sometimes you gotta learn to forgive and let things go. Hopefully, she learned her lesson. Man, you're hotheaded. She apologized and I accepted it. I'm moving on."

Caleb was generally a quiet person. We knew that he meant whatever he said. Everyone was silent on the way home.

In the silence, I thought about Caleb's words. It could be good that he chose to forgive her. I couldn't get what Jordan said about White people out of my mind. I think he was hotheaded about Ms. Meanie too.

When the car turned down our street, we could see Ms. Meanie's yard and a huge bin in the driveway, filled with ruined decorations. From Lee's drooping head I could tell he wished, just as much as I did, that we had not messed up Meanie's yard.

Finally, we reached home, where Mama greeted us with good news. "Your daddy's team won their basketball game. They are district champs," she said, smiling. "Y'all are quiet. How was your day?"

"Good," Lee and I said at the same time.

"How was the mall?"

"Good."

"Wow, y'all must be tired. We'll eat a small meal and both of you will go to bed. Sound like a plan?"

"Yes," we said, again at the same time.

Before we went to bed that night, I told Lee we should get on our knees to ask Jesus to forgive us and to help us make things good with Ms. Meanie.

"I was already thinking the same thing," he said. We went to our rooms. I felt much better after I prayed, and I had a good night's sleep.

It seemed like I was back at school in no time. As I sat next to Yanick in the classroom, my mind was full of thoughts about the mall and Ms. Meanie's yard. But I dropped all of that when Yanick asked, "Yo Ki, how come yuh neva wearin' de bracelet?"

My right hand grabbed my left wrist. I had forgotten to put it back on.

"Oh ... yes," I said. With the previous day's drama, I had forgotten to wear it that morning. I reached into my backpack, pulled out the box, and put it on my wrist.

"Wuh yuh seh? Yuh luv it? How come yuh nuh wearin' it?"

I struggled to respond. I didn't want to tell him the truth. At that moment, I couldn't find one good reason—or even a lie—for why I kept that beautiful bracelet hidden in my backpack. I was stuck.

Lee

6

Misunderstandings

I was tired in school. Even after Kiojah and I went to our rooms last night, I couldn't fall asleep. Mornings were rough for me. First of all, on cool mornings, sometimes my joints were stiff and sore. Second, I was not a morning person—I didn't like to talk, move, or think until about 10:30.

I started to wake up when Ms. Ferguson gave us time to work on our research projects. I was all in. That day, we gave each other feedback on our topics and the information we had found so far. While I worked with Fallon, Jordan walked behind her back, making faces. I ignored him.

"How was shopping last night? Did you find gifts for your parents?" she asked.

"Good. You know, if I had about a thousand dollars more, I would have definitely hooked them up with the best gifts," I said.

Fallon just laughed a little.

"But I can shop on a budget," I said quickly, taking out my cell phone while Ms. Ferguson wasn't watching. I showed Fallon the perfume we'd bought for Mama and the watch for Daddy.

"Nice," Fallon said.

Ellie, one of Fallon's sidekicks, walked up to us and asked, "Did you tell Lee about what your sister saw last night at the—?"

Fallon gave Ellie a mean look and she closed her mouth right away. Ugh. These girls bringing up the drama! I didn't have time for it.

"Oh yeah, Lee, it was all over FaceSpace and Snapblab, but it wasn't a good video," Fallon said. "My older sister said friends from her high school saw some drama in the perfume store at the mall with … Was it Jordan's brother? I mean, police officers were there, and like, he was about to get arrested. I know you guys were there. I mean, what went down?"

"Wait a minute, why do you think we were there?"

"Jordan blabbed about it yesterday, and like I think I saw you guys in that shaky video."

"Basically, a woman said Caleb did something he did not do. It was just because of the way he looks."

"What?"

"Another police officer and a secret shopper found the real thief. The woman at the perfume store saw that Jordan's brother was Black and was wearing high-top sneakers and torn jeans. She blamed him."

Fallon's face was questioning. "Well, was a Black guy stealing? Is it bad that the woman said Jordan's brother was stealing? A Black guy actually was taking things from the stores, right?"

Fallon's questions upset me, but I calmed myself down and replied, "Well, the problem was when the lady lied saying that she saw Jordan's brother take the perfume. She even said, 'you people always steal.' She thought Black people are all thieves. She hadn't even seen what had happened, because Caleb was *not* the thief."

Fallon just looked at me, blinking.

"It is a problem if White people think all Black people look alike," I said.

Again, Fallon just sat looking at me, blinking. "Um ... yeah. But I bet Black people do the same to White people if they are the same height and size or are wearing the same kind of clothes."

"Okay, team," Ms. Ferguson cut in. "It's time for you to switch and give feedback to a different teammate. Make sure you save enough time for both people to give a 'glow'—a compliment—and a 'grow'—how they can make it better. Remember, give the glow before you share the grow. When you hear the timer go off, it's the next person's turn to share before we rotate again. You guys are doing an amazing job of finding good information."

I looked at Fallon. As far as I was concerned, this topic was not over for us. There was so much she just didn't understand. Not all Black kids were bad, even though what we did to Ms. Meanie's yard could be one more reason White people would feel like we were.

The rest of the day was fuzzy to me.

On our way home, we saw Ms. Meanie putting up new lights and decorations. She was so busy that she didn't have time to tell us to "git" as if we were diseased dogs or something. Even though we were free to walk by peacefully, we didn't feel peace inside.

I took a nap, and when I woke up, it was nighttime. Daddy was home because he didn't have a game.

"Daddy, may I use the new laptop to design a T-shirt?" I asked.

"You can use the laptop for one hour. And I'd better not catch you up in the middle of the night working on anything."

I smiled. "Yes sir."

We sat down at the table for beef stew over rice with cornbread muffins. We all grabbed hands with the person next to us to bless our food.

"Lord, thank you for the vegetables. Thank you for the meat. Thank you for our family. Now let's eat," I prayed.

"So," Daddy said, breaking the quiet. "When I was driving home today, I noticed Ms. Lovett out in her yard putting up all her Christmas decorations again. I pulled over, but of course I didn't get out to stand on that white pavement. I asked her what was going on. She said some time last night she came outside to let her puppy out and was shocked by how messed up everything was in her yard. She said she even had to throw away some of her decorations."

"Wow!" Mama said. "I can't believe that. I mean, everyone knows Ms. Lovett is not the nicest person, but who would want to destroy her Christmas decorations?"

I was so ashamed. I wished I could just disappear. I didn't look at Kiojah because I knew it was just a matter of seconds before she would tell everything and before we'd be in a hot skillet. Once our parents got heated, no number of tears could put out the fire until we were punished—especially for something this bad.

Before we had a chance to tell our parents what we had done, Mama said, "Kiojah, why haven't you given that bracelet back to the boy?"

Kiojah's hand flew to her wrist. She was surprised that she had it on and did not say anything. We all knew that she struggled with telling the truth if she thought it would hurt someone else's feelings.

"You didn't tell him why you can't keep it?" Mama asked.

Kiojah faced the heat. She took off the bracelet and placed it on the table.

"Well, Ma ... I honestly don't understand why you don't want me to keep it. It doesn't make sense to me. He's a nice boy, and he gave me a nice gift. Why should I give it back? I don't get it."

I could tell Kiojah was scared to give it back to him and frustrated by the situation.

Mama stared and blinked for a few seconds. "Kiojah, don't raise your voice when you speak to me. This is why you can't keep the bracelet: You don't need a bracelet to be with someone you care about. If he likes being your friend, he doesn't need to give you a bracelet. You need to focus on school."

"I know. I just didn't want him to feel bad because his family is different. His mother doesn't care if he has a girlfriend."

"I know, Kiojah, but the more he understands you, the better friends the two of you can be."

"You're right, Ma. I guess I will tell him tomorrow in school."

"Yeah, honey, I believe that's best."

"Okay."

After I finished eating, I went to the laptop to start working on a logo for a club T-shirt. I thought about Caleb. I still thought it was amazing he just forgave that lady. Her whole face changed when she found out she was wrong about him.

I was tired of people thinking that just because I was a Black boy, I was going to do something bad. One time we were in a WalCare store, and Mama told Kiojah and me to pick a toy. I chose a rubber cell phone case. I walked around with the case looking for Kiojah, and a man followed me. He stopped me, took me to the front of the store, and said I was trying to steal the case.

"No, I told him to pick out one thing and I would buy it for him," Mama said when she came from the medicine counter. "You can't accuse him of stealing anything. We're still inside the store. I'm his mom, and I am paying for it." Mama turned to me and said, "Lee, put the case on the counter."

She grabbed our hands and we walked out of the store. Now, any time we go into that store, Mama tells us to stay with her and to always keep our hands out so people can see them.

I was getting sleepy, so I gave up working on the T-shirt design for the night.

7

The Truth
Will Set You Free

When we were getting into the car the next morning, I saw some new candy canes in Ms. Meanie's yard. I got so sad, once again, about Ms. Meanie and everything that had happened. As soon as Ma cranked up the car, I said, "Ma, I have something to tell you."

Lee raised his shoulders and dropped his head. He knew what I was going to say.

"Okay," Ma said, backing the car down the driveway.

"I know how Ms. Meanie's front yard got destroyed." Ma stopped the car in the middle of the driveway, shifting it into park.

"How?"

"Well, Jordan was upset because Ms. Meanie was always so rude to us," I started. Ma stared at me, pulling her neck back and dropping her chin towards her chest. "He came up with the idea for us to destroy the lights and the decorations." Ma's chin came forward and her eyes got big. "It was his way to shut her up so that she would leave us alone." Ma's mouth dropped open.

"Kiojah, you and Lee helped do that? I am *so* disappointed."

I could tell Ma was furious and she was thinking about what to do. I hated this because I always wanted to please my parents. I loved them so much. I cared about what they thought of me.

"I don't have time to go to Ms. Lovett's house right now, but you know I will," Ma said, shifting the car back into reverse. "I have to tell your daddy. Y'all knew better than that. Why did you think it was okay to do that?"

Looking straight ahead, she said, "Listening to Jordan ...?"

Lee always said he knew when Mama was hot because she talked to herself without letting anyone else say a word.

"You say she was mean? If she was saying stuff to you every day, why didn't y'all just tell Nana or me? I would have loved to have gone down to talk to her about it. Now I have to go and tell her what I'm going to do to your behinds."

We could forget about going to any games or doing anything fun on the weekend.

"You will stay home with Nana this weekend. If she can't watch you, I'll stay home myself."

This didn't bother me as much as it hurt Lee. He looked forward to doing new things and traveling to new places. For me, being at home and watching TV with Nana was just fine.

Mama was not playing around. She remembered everything. Once when Lee got in trouble for talking too much in class, she said he couldn't go on a trip to a water park with our church's children's group. The trip was three weeks away, but when the time came, she didn't forget. Guess where Lee was while we were at Aqua Blast Water Park! He was at home with Mama, doing his homework, cleaning his room, and working with Daddy in the yard.

Listening to Jordan was the worst decision.

"If she's just a mean old lady," Mama continued, "could you not have ignored her? Sometimes old people are mean because they're sick or lonely. They say her husband died about five years ago, and she's never been the same. I'll tell you this—your daddy and I did not teach you to do evil for evil. When somebody is mean to you, you need to stand up for yourself in the right way. Then you need to forgive them."

The rest of the ride to school was silent. When the car pulled up to the front circle, we said, "I love you Ma."

"I love you too," she replied in a voice that sounded more sad than angry.

Lee and I didn't say a word as we walked to class. I knew I had done the right thing by telling the truth. So, why did doing the right thing feel so wrong? We turned the corner and saw Jordan. Could my morning have gotten any worse? I had hoped I could at least get through the morning without Jordan knowing that I told Mama everything.

"Mornin'," Jordan said with all his sass.

"Hey, Jordan."

Lee looked at me with a sly smile and squinted his eyes.

"Jordan, you know Kiojah can't hold the beans," he said.

Jordan twisted around with his hand on his hip, looked at me, and then looked back at Lee. Jordan and his drama!

"What you mean, Lee? She spilled the water?" he asked with even more sass.

"No," I said. "Both of you are saying it wrong. It's 'can't hold water' or 'spilled the beans.'" I was upset because they were talking about me as if I wasn't there.

"Man, on the way to school before we could even back out of the driveway, Kiojah was in tears and told Mama everything," Lee said. "I mean, *e-ver-y-thing* about what we did to Ms. Meanie's house that night before we went to the mall."

"Girl, you are sooo … ooh …" Jordan said, trying not to say what he thought of me at that moment.

"It was the right thing to do," I said. "I couldn't keep hearing Mama talk about how terrible Meanie's yard looked and not tell her the truth."

"Well, you coulda not told her the truth 'bout me and Lee. You coulda said you did it yourself!" Jordan huffed as he spoke.

We laughed.

"Now, Jordan, you know I did the right thing."

For the next two minutes, until we got to the classroom, we listened while Jordan told me twenty reasons why I should not have told my mom about tearing up Ms. Meanie's yard.

Class was just starting when we walked in. Ms. Ferguson had the morning work on the board. The classroom was quiet. I saw that Yanick was not in his seat. A few minutes later, the door opened, and he walked in with a drink from a coffee shop.

"Gud mawnin'," he said, giving a note to Ms. Ferguson.

"Good morning, Yanick. Please put your drink on my desk. We are finishing up bell work, and we're about to start our language arts lesson."

I picked up the books for our literacy circle and passed them out. When I reached out to give a book to Yanick, he noticed that I didn't have on the bracelet. Again.

All the drama made me forget to put the bracelet back on.

"Ki gyal, how come yuh nuh wearin' de bracelet? Yuh can tell me now." Usually Yanick was smiling, but this time his face looked confused.

I unzipped my backpack and pulled out the jewelry box. As I was about to open it to put on the bracelet, I suddenly felt brave. My morning couldn't get any worse. I had nothing to lose. I looked him in the eyes, and said, "Every day I have been hiding the bracelet in my backpack because my mom told me to give it back to you. It's an awesome gift, but I can't keep it. I'm not allowed to take gifts from boys."

Yanick looked confused, but he nodded his head and said, "Me undastand yuh now."

"I hope we're still friends."

"Everyting irie."

I smiled at him. I felt good, but at the same time, I felt like my mom treated me like a little girl compared to the way other parents treated their kids. I mean, we just got cell phones in fifth grade.

Yanick bent over, unzipped the front of his backpack, and put the little box inside. He acted like nothing had happened. It was so easy that I wished I had told him sooner. I was thankful he said we could still be friends.

I felt so much better that I had told Mama and Yanick the truth.

Later that morning Ms. Ferguson took us to the music room. We saw some huge grasshopper bugs that had been on the wall for days.

"I thank this green grasshopper would look nice on Areebah's red shirt," Jimmie said, walking over to a big bug that was chillin' on the wall. Actually, the bug was so chill that it looked like it was dead.

"Aaahh!" Areebah screamed, and we all jumped up.

"Bring that thing close to me and I'll chop your arm in half like it was a pretzel stick," Areebah said when she finally stopped screaming and hiding behind Ms. Ferguson.

Kids were either screaming, because Jimmie had picked up the grasshopper, or laughing, because they were not afraid of bugs and Areebah was beyond scared. Even Ms. Ferguson was laughing.

"Okay, okay, team," she said as her face became serious. "Let's get settled before we enter the music room. We can't go in to see Mr. Alvarez if we're carrying on this way. Give me five."

The whole class, except for Jordan, gave her a high five. Ms. Ferguson stared at Jordan and spread her fingers wider. Jordan put up his hand, stood straight and tall, and closed his mouth. Mr. Alvarez came out and led us into his classroom, where music was already playing.

We danced our way to our spots on the big carpet in front of the board.

"Good afternoon. Today we will continue our rehearsal for the winter concert. It will be in a couple weeks, just before you go on break," he said, turning down the music.

I loved school concerts. The best part was dressing up and having our parents come out to see us perform. Two weeks earlier, Lee had tried out for a solo in front of the whole fifth grade. He handled his business! Lee was one of the best singers at our school, and we were about to find out who had been chosen.

"I would like the following students to come and stand in front of the classroom: Alera Mincey, Ellie Stephan, Lee Hughes, Rashad Holmes, Jordan Smith, and Morgen Gainey."

Our whole team cheered.

"Okay, okay. Let's settle down," Mr. Alvarez said. "The two students from this class who will lead the fifth grade are ..."

Lee

Your True Colors
Shine Through

"Lee Hughes and Ellie Stephan! Please give it up for all your classmates," Mr. Alvarez said, clapping his hands.

Everyone cheered again. I reached out to fist-bump Kiojah as I walked back to my seat.

At the end of the class, Ms. Ferguson showed up. "I'm waiting for a nice, quiet line so that you can go to lunch. It's your lunchtime you're wasting. If you miss lunch, I could always just get a few of those grasshoppers, take them into the classroom, and divide them up."

Everyone lost it and screamed, *"Nooo!"*

"I have salt, pepper, and hot sauce," she said, trying to look serious.

Everybody laughed. Ms. Ferguson smiled quietly and waved goodbye to Mr. Alvarez.

When we got back to the classroom, Kiojah told me she had given the bracelet back to Yanick.

"Good for you," I said. I knew it was hard for her, but Yanick would be okay. By recess that day, he was more than okay.

Tall trees shaded the area where Luke and Jimmie were swinging on the monkey bars. Areebah and I sat down under the branches to hide ourselves from the burning sun overhead. As soon as we settled, we saw Yanick on the other side of the playground near the slides, beside the swings.

"Who is he talking to?" I asked, leaning to try to get a better look at what he was doing.

"Is that—?" Areebah said as the girl stood up from a swing.

"Fallon!" we whispered out loud at the same.

Good thing Kiojah and Jordan were out in the field running laps for the jogging club! Yanick put his hand in his pocket, pulled out the same box he had given Kiojah, and gave it to Fallon.

Areebah's mouth dropped. "Ugh!" she gasped as her eyes opened wide.

I shook my head. "No!"

Areebah pointed her finger and started to stand up.

I grabbed her arm and pushed her finger down. "It's not worth it," I said.

We watched a little bit longer to make sure it

was the same bracelet. Fallon took it out and held it up. Yep! It was the same rose gold charm bracelet.

I was so happy that Kiojah had given that brace-let back to Yanick. I wished she had never accepted it in the first place.

"Man, Kiojah would be so upset if she knew that Yanick gave the bracelet to someone else on the same day that she gave it back to him," Areebah said, shaking her head.

I had a feeling that Kiojah was going to be all right. As we stood up, we saw that Fallon had the bracelet on her arm.

"Now I know Kiojah is gonna see that bracelet," Areebah said.

"Maybe not," I said. "I'm not telling her until after school. No need to ruin her day."

Back in class, we had a science session. I lived for this, because we could move around to different stations in pairs. I wasn't a science dude, but I liked the labs.

Ms. Ferguson played music while we shifted from one station to another. I got loose every now and then if she played one of my songs. We had a good time. Before we knew it, we heard the explo-sion. Ms. Ferguson had a rocket sound on her timer. The blast let us know time was up.

"Hey team, it's time to clean up your stations," she said.

I could not believe this dramatic day was already over. I wondered what would happen on our walk home when we had to pass by Ms. Meanie. Had Ma already told Daddy what we had done? Did they talk to Ms. Meanie ... or the police? I wished I had never agreed with Jordan's idea.

"Okay, team, pack up. I'll be at the door for a handshake, a high five, or a hug," Ms. Ferguson announced.

We lined up with our backpacks, lunch boxes, and jackets. Most of the team hugged Ms. Ferguson because we loved her. Some of us had been with her for two years in a row because she'd changed to the fifth grade this year.

Like every day, Jordan, Kiojah, and I hugged Ms. Nina before we crossed the street, but today was different because none of us was talking.

Finally, Kiojah said, "Hey guys, I'm sorry if I got us in trouble when I told Mama the truth. I was feeling so bad about what we did."

We could tell Kiojah was waiting for us to say something. We didn't, so she kept talking.

"I had to say something because I saw the police and heard Ms. Meanie crying, and Ma and Daddy talked about it at dinner."

As we turned the corner, we saw Daddy's truck parked in front of Ms. Meanie's yard. He was talking to her. I wasn't surprised. He could talk to anybody, especially about sports. He was smiling and laughing with Ms. Meanie, and she was actually being … nice.

When Daddy saw us, he stopped talking and he stopped smiling. The walk to Ms. Meanie's bright white sidewalk seemed extra long.

"You two are mine," Daddy said, pointing to Kiojah and me. "So, you know what's waiting for you at home. Jordan, my wife already called your mother." He looked at all of us and said, "So, what do you all think you owe Ms. Lovett?"

Jordan said, "Who …?" but Kiojah grabbed his arm. We knew he was about to ask, "Who is Ms. Lovett?"

Of course, Kiojah was the first to say something. She apologized with her mouth and her eyes at the same time.

"Ms. Mean—! I mean Ms. Lovett … we are so sorry we ripped down your lights and busted up your Santa and snapped your candy canes and put all that dirt on your driveway," Kiojah said in tears.

Well, Kiojah had said it all, so Jordan and I just stood there, waiting for what would happen next. What did happen surprised all of us. Ms. Meanie—oops, I mean Ms. Lovett—started to cry. I never knew a mean witch could make tears. No one said anything. Not even Daddy.

Finally, Jordan said, "Your yard is the nicest one in the neighborhood. We were just ticked off because you don't like us to walk on your sidewalk. I was hot, but I didn't think about how destroying your yard would make you feel."

Daddy looked at me, I guessed because I hadn't said anything yet.

"We are sorry," I said. "We can help you, even though it seems like you have most of the decorations back in place. Maybe we can help you take them down after Christmas."

Daddy cut in. "Maybe you all can work to earn money to pay Ms. Lovett back for the money she had to spend on new decorations for her yard."

Ms. Lovett just cried and cried. We stared at each other. She pulled a small towel out of her pocket and blew her nose.

"You children did not deserve me being so mean to you," she said. "I should be happy to see you pass by my house, because most days I'm lonely. My grandchildren are about your age. I miss them so much." She blew her nose again and wiped her tears. "They moved away about three years ago, about the same time my husband died. It's been so hard to be here alone."

We stood with our mouths open. I could see that Jordan really felt bad. What happened next surprised me.

Jordan said, "Ms. Mean—I mean, Ms. Lovett—I know you feel alone, but you're not alone. We can be your grandkids. You should come to our holiday concert to hear Lee sing."

My mouth dropped down to the tops of my sneakers. Kiojah elbowed me because my face was about to fall through the earth. Even though Jordan's head could be hard, he also knew how to love hard.

"Because, girl, I like this white sidewalk," he said. "I think instead of just pink you could add a little bit more color to your house."

We all laughed.

Ms. Lovett said, "Oh really?"

"Yaaass. Lee knows how to put colors together. We can upgrade you. Take it to the next level!" Jordan said.

Kiojah was smiling, and I knew we were probably going to be a lot more than friends with Ms. Lovett. She was so excited about having new 'grandkids.'

"Oh, you children have got to try the new recipe I have for hot chocolate, and I just baked cinnamon rolls this afternoon. After your supper tonight, see if you can come back here."

"Yes ma'am," we all said at the same time.

"Is that all right with you, Daddy?" I asked.

"Of course," he said.

Kiojah, Jordan, and I each gave Ms. Lovett a hug ... and she hugged us back.

Yanick's Glossary: Jamaican Patois to English

Jamaican Patois is known locally as Patois and called Jamaican Creole by linguists.

Page	Jamaican Patois	English
4	Tanks	Thanks
5	We moved up yah fram down sout. We live in de apartments right acrass de street fram River Forest.	We moved up here from down south. We live in the apartments right across the street from River Forest.
5	Me family originally fram Jamrock. Me taak Patois an English."	My family is originally from Jamaica. I speak Patois and English.
5	Jamrock. Yuh know? Jamaica. Now me mudda is a student at de university yah. Kiojah, weh yuh seh?"	Jamrock. You know? Jamaica. Now my mother is a student at the university here. Kiojah, what are you saying?
6	Neva	Never
7	Ki, me wanna tank yuh for helpin' today. May me call yuh Ki?	Ki, I want to thank you for helping me today. May I call you Ki?

7	Me feelin' dis school, yuh know.	I'm feeling this school, you know.
8	Wah gwan twin?	What's going on, twin? How are you, twin? What's up, twin?
25	Wah gwan, Ki?	What's going on, Ki? How are you, Ki? What's up, Ki?
25	How yuh likin' de bracelet?	How are you liking the bracelet?
29	Tek care, Ki.	Take care, Ki.
51	Yo Ki, how come yuh neva wearin' de bracelet?	Yo Ki, how come you never wear the bracelet?
51	Wuh yuh seh? Yuh luv it? How come yuh nuh wearin' it?	What do you say? You love it? How come you don't wear it?
65	Gud mawnin'	Good morning.
66	Ki gyal, how come yuh nuh wearin' de bracelet? Yuh can tell me now.	Ki girl, how come you're not wearing the bracelet? You can tell me now.
66	Me undastand yuh now.	Now I understand you.
66	Everyting irie.	Everything is okay. Everything is all right.

About the Author

KECIA A. JOHNSON was born and raised and still resides in Gainesville, Florida. Inspired by her experiences with students as a middle school reading teacher, K-12 writing coach, and elementary and high school media specialist, she decided to explore storytelling and creative writing. She was drawn to students who were reluctant to engage in literacy activities because they struggled in those areas. The encouragement from five friends, support from family, and divine inspiration led her to write and publish The Kiojah and Lee Book Series. She hopes her books will give children positive experiences with literature, a good laugh, and something to talk about. She holds a BS in journalism and an MA in mass communication with concentrations in writing for print news and multimedia storytelling from the University of Florida.